A**ʜ**

& Other
Stories

The Artist

DISCLAIMER: "This is a work of fiction. Names, characters, places and incidents are products of the author's imagination and are used fictitiously. Any resemblance to actual events, locales or persons, living or dead, is entirely coincidental."

Copyright © 2018 P. J. Blakey-Novis

All rights reserved.

Cover Design by Red Cape Graphic Design

www.redcapepublishing.com

DEDICATION

For all those who have supported my writing, provided feedback, bought my books, and left reviews. Especially Leanne, for reading everything in its early stages, for believing in my work, and for creating all my promotional posts.

ABOUT THE AUTHOR

This is the third collection of short horror stories from author P.J. Blakey-Novis. Peter lives with his wife and four children in a small town in Sussex, England. As well as being a keen cook and wine enthusiast, Peter has been writing poetry and short stories for almost twenty years. An excitement for literature and storytelling has led to Peter publishing two novels, three collections of short stories, and a children's book, to date.

KEEP UP TO DATE!

More information about the author can be found on his publisher's website as well as social media profiles listed below. You can also subscribe to the email mailing list via the website for exciting news about future releases, as well as accessing short stories direct to your mailbox! If you have any comments or would like to just get in touch feel free to email directly at the address below. Happy reading!

Twitter:
www.twitter.com/pjbn_author
Facebook:
www.facebook.com/pjbnauthor
Instagram:
www.instagram.com/pjbn_author
Pinterest:
www.pinterest.co.uk/redcapepublishing
Web:
www.redcapepublishing.com/book-shop
Email:
redcapepublishing@outlook.com

CONTENTS

The Artist

The Children of the Deep

The Confessional

Meredith

Unearthed

Wash Away Your Sins

THE ARTIST

Everyone told me that I was gifted from a young age. I must have been about four or five when I first picked up a set of pencils and began to sketch. Straight lines were easy, so I drew incredibly detailed pictures of my bedroom to begin with. Each piece of furniture was meticulously brought to life. I spent days on each image. I'd take the drawings into school to show off to my teachers, who rewarded me with compliments and stickers.

It wasn't until I began secondary school, when Art became its own lesson, that my talent began to be talked about with more excitement. The Art faculty at my school was small, made up of only two teachers. In my first year of secondary school I was taught by Mr. Low, a man in his late sixties who was happy to have his students painting pictures of fruit, or simple landscapes. He gave the impression, which may well have been very

The Artist

accurate, that he did not expect much from his students. Perhaps this was why I stood out. While my classmates were happy to soak the paper in paint, lines of green for the grass, blue for the sky, and a yellow splodge for the sun, I would create pieces that were almost photographic in their quality.

Mr. Low said I was an A-grade student, a talented kid. Nevertheless, he explained that I needed to focus on more useful subjects, or else I'd end up as an Art teacher. To me, that sounded like a great career choice, but the disappointment in his voice suggested otherwise. Drawing and painting were what I loved, and I was determined to make a future out of it. I could never have imagined just what form that would take, or the damage my choices would do.

"How do you make a living as an artist?" I asked him, at the end of one lesson when my classmates had left the room. He looked at me sadly.

"Create a lot of works and be dead. The big money only really

The Artist

comes posthumously. Or learn to paint portraits. There is a market for portraits still, and it's only the wealthy that could buy them."

The first school year went by quickly, with all my spare time sketching in the book I carried on me at all times. I took books from the library which claimed to teach one how to draw people. Too shy to ask anyone to sit for me, I copied people from magazines, film posters, even pausing the television and drawing the news reporters. As with most things in life, the more I practiced, the better I became.

A week before the start of the summer break, I decided to sketch Mr. Low, from his photograph on the school's website. It turned out well, my best so far, and I knew that he would be pleased with it. Even his profile photo looked sad. I didn't know much about him, not really. He wore a wedding ring but had never talked about his life outside of school. *I wish you could have made it as an artist,* I mumbled as I looked at my portrait. I scribbled a signature at the bottom before

The Artist

rolling it up and securing it with an elastic band. I was right that Mr. Low would like the picture; he seemed genuinely impressed with it.

"Where do you think you will put it?" I asked, eagerly.

"I have a little studio in my garage, where I paint. It can go in there."

"I'd like to see your paintings some time," I replied with sincerity.

"You can," he said. "There are a few seascapes in the pub near the beach. They've been there a few years now, not that anyone has ever bought any."

"Sir," I began. "I'm twelve. I don't tend to go to the pub." Mr. Low looked at me a little puzzled.

"Of course, yes. Well, maybe your parents can take you in to see the paintings one day."

It was a couple of weeks into the summer break when we first headed to the beach. My dad was working most days, so it was just my mum, Jenny (my little sister), and myself. The beach is only a twenty-minute walk from our house

The Artist

and would have been lazy to drive there, mum said. Of course, at my age I was unfamiliar with the pubs and hadn't thought much more about what Mr. Low had told me. Now I saw it, though. As we turned the last corner approaching the beach, there was the pub that he had mentioned to me.

"Can we go in the pub?" I asked. Mum looked at me a little surprised. We didn't go to pubs; it just wasn't the sort of place that our parents took us.

"Why on earth do you want to go to the pub?"

"My art teacher has some paintings in there. He said to have a look if I could."

"They have a tree house with a slide around the back," Jenny piped up. Mum looked bewildered.

"Now, how do you know that?" she asked.

"Rachel's mum took us here last week, when I went around to play."

"Did she now?" Mum mumbled. "OK, I'll tell you what. Let's get an orange juice each and

The Artist

sit out the back for a little bit. You can see the paintings and have a little play. Then we get to the beach before the tide starts coming back in."

"Can I have wine?" Jenny asked.

"No, you're eight. Ten more years." With that, we made our way inside. Mum ordered three orange juices, before asking how to get out to the garden. I scanned the walls, finding no paintings. There were rectangular marks on the paintwork, as though the sunlight had not reached them, as if something had been hung there until recently. I pulled at mum's sleeve.

"I can't see the paintings." Mum glanced around. "Can you ask someone?"

"Excuse me," she said, looking at the barmaid who had served our drinks. "My son's art teacher told him he had some paintings here on display?"

"All gone, I'm afraid. Someone bought them all."

The Artist

"Well, there you go," Mum told me.

"That can't be right. He said he never sold any!" The barmaid looked at me.

"They were here for quite a while. Probably a tourist coming through with money to burn."

When the time came to return to school, I couldn't wait to talk to Mr. Low. I knew he'd be happy that he had sold the paintings, but he wasn't there. All the school office would tell me was that he had resigned. I didn't know where he lived, or how to contact him, and I could have cried. It was three days before we had our first art lesson, and I was anxious about who would be taking the class.

"My name is Miss Starlight," she announced as we took to our seats. We all knew her name, as she had been the other half of the art faculty, but no-one actually believed that Starlight was her real name. Most of the male students referred to her as the 'hot hippie', whilst the female students complained about

The Artist

the injustice of not being allowed to dye their hair whilst the art teacher sported bright blue dreadlocks. "As some of you may know, Mr. Low is no longer working here. I will be taking your art lessons until a replacement is found."

"Why did he leave?" I blurted out, uncharacteristically talking in front of the class.

"You sad 'cos your boyfriend left?" Matthew said, causing a wave of laughter. My fondness for Mr. Low had been the subject of mockery before, and I had done my best to ignore it, but Matthew was an unpleasant individual.

"Actually, he had a rather good reason. An art dealer approached him and has purchased all his paintings, with the intention of buying more. He has decided to focus on this, instead of teaching. Anyway, on with the lesson. For the next few weeks we are going to focus on expressionism, and you are to draw, paint, or sculpt, a piece which represents one of your classmates. I'll be choosing who is paired with whom at random. Now, the piece of work can be anything you like; you may draw something as lifelike as possible, or shapes and colours that the person brings to mind. It really is down to you."

"Can I be paired with Claire?" Matthew asked. Everyone looked at him, confused by the request. Claire was even less popular than me; obese, with glasses and ginger hair - the easiest of victims for a bully. "That way, I can just draw a ginger blob, and it will be spot-on." There was laughter again, but not from me. I fixed Matthew with a glare, my anger at his cruelty overpowering my usual cowardice. Claire began to sob, which only added to the laughter from Matthew and his group.

"That's a detention for you," Miss Starlight said, trying to conceal her own contempt for the boy. "No-one will want to work with you if you treat people like that." Miss Starlight pulled a brown envelope out from her desk drawer. "In here I have everyone's names. I'll pull out two at a time, and those people will be working together for this project.

The Artist

It's not optional, so I suggest you all make the best of it. And if anyone creates something that I deem to be malicious, there will be consequences."

I didn't honestly care who I got put with; I could draw anyone so would just do it as accurately as possible. Even so, it was pretty rotten luck that I got paired with Matthew. My first instinct was to draw a very detailed dick picture, deep purple veins, a bulbous head spewing out semen which looked like speech bubbles from a comic. I could then fill in text with all the nasty stuff he said on a daily basis. I grinned without realising I was doing so.

"Something funny?" Matthew asked.

"Nope," I lied. I knew I wouldn't actually draw what I wanted to, but it made me feel better to know I *could*, if I was just a little braver. Instead, I concentrated on drawing Matthew as skilfully as I could, all the while dreading what he would come up with. The class seemed, much to Miss Starlight's surprise, to take to the task quite well. The room was quiet; only the sounds of pencils and brushes against paper could be heard. By the time the bell rang to signify the end of class, I had made good progress with the outline of Matthew's face.

"How's yours going?" I asked him.

"You'll see when it's finished." He gave me a smile that made me nervous. Looking back, it was probably a mistake on Miss Starlight's part to finish the project by getting each of us to stand before the class and hold up our work, certainly without her checking the pieces first. When the time came, at the end of the third lesson on this project, we were called up to show what we had done. I suppose that mine was as expected; very good as sketches go, clearly a picture of who I was assigned to draw. Black and white pencil shading, on a sheet of A3 sized paper. Matthew shuffled a few sheets of A4 as he stood up, winking at me.

The Artist

"I'm not very good at drawing, Miss," he explained. "So, I came up with something that I think represents the subject well." I felt my stomach turn as I watched him apply sticky tape to the sheets, fixing them against the white board. "It's like a comic, Miss. So you may have to come closer to see it properly." Matthew's mates jumped up first, knowing that they needed to get a look before the teacher did. Their howls of laughter told me that I didn't want to see, but I couldn't help myself, and just made it before Miss Starlight ripped them down. It was nothing but a series of stickman drawings, the first featuring (presumably) me giving a picture to a taller stickman with grey hair (presumably Mr. Low). This was followed by the pair of us in various positions, I didn't catch them all, but in one Mr. Low had me bent over his desk as I said 'thank-you'. I wasn't surprised by Matthew's 'work', but I knew it would something that was talked about for a long time; teenagers could be an unforgiving bunch.

The Artist

Of course, Matthew would be punished, and the pictures destroyed, but that wouldn't make much difference. I tried not to react, but I felt my face redden, and became desperate not to cry. I felt powerless, and this is perhaps the worst feeling in the world. Miss Starlight kept me behind after class that day, wanting to check that I was alright. I pretended that I was, and there was little more that she could have done.

"For what it's worth," she began, "you'll be getting a good mark for the drawing. It really is excellent." I looked at it, anger burning in my eyes.

"I wish he would go away," I told Miss Starlight. "If only he would break a leg or something, anything to keep him away from here for a while." The teacher stayed silent for a moment.

"Are you OK walking home? I don't want any trouble outside of school if Matthew is still about." I hadn't thought about this, but I rarely saw them outside of school as we lived in opposite direction, so I

The Artist

said I'd be fine and made my way out across the car park. There are two exits from the school, and I take the one to the left which leads on to the new-build housing estate that I live on. But something pulled me in the other direction that day, a sound of commotion, the flickering of blue lights reflected in the windows of parked cars, so I made my way towards the growing group of teenagers and passers-by. At the back of the crowd I spotted Claire and asked her what was going on. She grinned at me.

"Matthew got run over!" she whispered, a little too excitedly. "He's not dead or anything, but his leg looks pretty mashed up. It snapped the wrong way at the knee." I felt sick; I knew my face had gone pale, and my legs felt odd. I didn't reply to Claire, just turned and headed towards home. *If only he would break a leg or something.* My words came back to haunt me. *Coincidence!* I told myself. I couldn't stop thinking about it for the rest of the day, all the way up to falling asleep. At three in the morning I

The Artist

woke up, suddenly, and was hit by another thought. *I wish you could have made it as an artist.* I couldn't get back to sleep after that, my logical brain telling me that I was being stupid.

Climbing out of bed and switching on the lamp on my desk, I grabbed a pencil and paper. I looked around for inspiration, my eyes falling on a photograph of Jenny taken at a dance show. Quickly, I began sketching her; it wasn't my best work, but the resemblance was obvious.

"Wake up, and come to my room," I said to the picture, feeling more than a little silly. I sat in my chair, holding my breath, listening out for signs of movement. And then it came; little footsteps down the hallway, my bedroom door creaking open. My heart raced, wanting to believe this was a coincidence but knowing it could not be. Jenny stood there holding her stuffed rabbit, rubbing at her eyes.

"What's up?" I asked. She looked around, clearly confused.

The Artist

"Nothing. Sorry, I don't know. Must have been dreaming." I sent her back to bed, my mind reeling. The possibilities were endless, if not a little terrifying, but there had to be some limitations to this supposed power; I just had no way to fully grasp it. I drew mum, told the picture that she should give me £10 in the morning to buy sweets with. If this worked, then there was no way that it was coincidence. Mum never bought sweets, and she never gave us money for ourselves.

At 7.30am I was on my way to school, a crisp ten-pound note in my pocket, and a list of ways I could improve the world swirling around in my mind. I felt a little guilt over Matthew's accident, but only a little, and at that time I never considered using this power to hurt people. I still don't know how I reached this point.

Over the rest of my school years, I felt invincible. I drew Claire next, telling her to exercise regularly and eat better. And she did; by the following school year she was of an average size, and her confidence had much improved. She even got a boyfriend, albeit a nerdy guy with greasy hair and horrific acne. I drew bullies, and they soon had minor accidents. Nothing like the broken leg Matthew suffered, which took almost six months to heal, but little things like tripping over in front of people or urinating themselves during school plays. I fantasised about winning the lottery as I turned old enough to buy a ticket but couldn't figure out a way to make that happen, so resorted to telling people to give me things. It started with my parents, of course, from that time I told my mum to give me ten pounds for sweets, but I started to feel what I assume was guilt. A while after this, I started drawing some of the kids I didn't like and told them to bring me money. By the time I was seventeen, I had ten kids at school each giving me £20 daily. I didn't know where they were getting it, and I didn't care. I was getting greedy.

The Artist

At eighteen, and still a virgin, I used my power to get laid. I'm not proud of it, but I did it. It also wasn't all that good, but I had the pick of the school and despite all being over much quicker than I had hoped, I did get to see a beautiful girl naked. I felt guilty afterward, more so than I had over any of my other actions, as though I had forced it to happen. I suppose I did, in fact. I vowed to never do it again, but hormones, and my lack of any genuine offers, meant that I could not be trusted in this way. Soon I had slept with a number of young women, all of whom believed it had been their idea, so no one was really hurt by my actions.

Until Madison. The girls before her had been conquests; a display of my new-found power, and the fulfilment of my urges. Madison was different, and we were together a number of times. I was getting better at doing the deed, and I started to fall for her. I told the drawing of her to come and find me for sex, and she would. I told the drawing to love me, for her to be

The Artist

with me, and she did. We were perfect together, although no-one could understand what she saw in me, including herself. I left all the drawings alone, apart from hers, and for a year we spent all our time with each other.

I had several drawings of her, in varying stages of undress, stuck to my bedroom wall. I would talk to them, tell them what I wanted. Aside from the sexual side of the relationship, I simply told her to love me, to stay with me for all time. My exact words were 'until death do us part'. I thought it was a reasonably request; I knew I could be good to her and although it may have been somewhat false, she would have believed herself to be happy with me. I was naive. I thought love was possible at such a young age, but it was merely an illusion. I could control people's actions, that much was clear. But perhaps it was too much to control how they honestly felt? Maybe it only worked when we were together?

After our first year together, I heard a rumour about another guy

The Artist

that Madison had been seeing. I didn't believe it; I couldn't see how it would be possible if she loved me. So, I asked her outright, and she began to cry.

"I'm sorry," she told me. "This thing between us is weird, and I can't take it anymore. You know, I don't even think about you when I'm not here. I just suddenly get the urge to see you; it's as if it's out of my hands. I can't explain it. I told my friend, and she said you've hypnotized me or something. That I wouldn't go for you out of choice."

"You have to stay with me," I said, almost pleading.

"Look at me, not those fucking drawings, when you say that!" she said. "You can't make me stay." Madison turned to leave, intending to walk out of my life forever, but I couldn't let that happen.

"Sit down!" I said, commanding the pencil drawing of her face. Madison sat, a little surprised at her own actions. Something in me changed in that moment, a desire to show off how powerful I was, a need for revenge

The Artist

against my love that had forsaken me. "I can make you do anything I please," I told her. She looked afraid but did not try to move. "Watch."

"Take off your top," I told the picture. Madison began to undress, but it was clear that she did not want to; her hands were obeying me, but her mind was trying to fight it. "See?" I asked. She did not reply, just stared at me through widened eyes, struggling to process what was happening.

"I told you that you were to stay with me, until death did us part. That's not something we can change. But I don't know if I can forgive you for betraying me. Are you even sorry?"

"Not at all," she said, defiantly. "You're fucking crazy!" I didn't mean to say what came next.

"Then we're finished. And you are so upset that you can't go on living any longer. Now get out!" Madison looked at me as if I were insane, hastily putting her top back on, before walking out and slamming the door behind her. I broke down in tears at the loss of

The Artist

my love, and over what I knew was now inevitable.

News broke the next day of Madison's suicide, a bathtub filled with crimson water, deep slices down each of her forearms. The note she left blamed me, and rightly so, but everyone assumed it was because I had ended our relationship. I had gone too far, and although I had no intention in following in Madison's footsteps, I knew that I needed to get this power under control. I thought back over the last few years and the wasted opportunity to use my talent for the good of others. Greed and lust had been my downfall, and had ended in death. I knew I could never draw again, but doubted I had the willpower to resist.

I considered breaking my fingers, or pounding my hands with a hammer, but feared they would heal in time. There was only one way to be certain that I never drew again, one way to make sure I could not look at another picture and control that person. I searched

The Artist

through the draw of my desk until I came across my fountain pen; an unused gift from my dad for my eighteenth birthday. I took a deep breath before plunging it as quickly as I could into my right eye, the pain far more excruciating than I had expected. *Don't stop,* I told myself, ramming it into my left eye and twisting, causing a wet sensation to run down my face. I tried to look around but could see nothing; it worked. Finally, everyone was safe.

THE CHILDREN OF THE DEEP

I could begin to tell this story by suggesting I enjoyed going for long walks at night. That, perhaps, would be a strange activity to take part in. The truth is that I would regularly walk home from a drinking session, having missed the last bus, busy with those final few shots. There were pubs nearer to my home than the one I chose to frequent, but they were either less pleasant venues, or had priced me out. As a result, I made The Traveller's Rest my regular hide-out; a traditional British pub in which every surface was sticky, and one could still detect the odour of stale tobacco smoke, despite smoking in pubs having been banned back in 2006. However, to its merit, The Traveller's drinks were priced in a way more suited to my budget, and the pub featured a beer garden which overlooked the English Channel. In fact, due to the erosion of the local coastline, the pub was now

The Artist

positioned a little too close to the cliff edge for comfort, and staff were known to escort especially inebriated customers out to taxis to ensure they didn't wander the wrong way and end up mashed on the rocks below.

June 1st was a typical Friday evening for me, aside from the air temperature being a good ten degrees warmer than usual. Perhaps this was to be the start of the fabled British summer; heat we are unaccustomed to, complain about, then miss terribly when it disappears a fortnight later. On this particular Friday, I had finished work in the nearest city, where I had been cooped up in a call-centre all day trying (unsuccessfully) to sell life insurance, and alighted the bus outside The Traveller's Rest. It was on the route which took me home, which was convenient, but the walk back afterwards would be a good forty minutes, or more, depending on how much I drank. And I drank a lot.

This evening played out the same as so many before; I arrived at

The Artist

the bar around 6pm, I ordered two pints of strong scrumpy, two double whiskeys, and made my way out to the garden. I always ordered two of each drink, as the first one would go down too quickly, and I hated having to queue at the bar. Thankfully, my usual table was clear. I headed there out of habit now, having soon learned that it was the only outside table which didn't wobble if you leaned on it. I gazed out across the stillness of the Channel, knocking back the drinks, and making my way through almost an entire twenty-pack of Superkings. I lost track of time as I made my way back from the bar to my table with my twelfth pint of scrumpy and had just sat (rather heavily) back down when I heard the bell ring for 'time at the bar'. I knew I had maybe ten to fifteen minutes to finish my drink, before one of the bar staff would remind me I needed to go home. I also knew that the last bus home had left almost half an hour ago.

It may have been the heat, which didn't mix well with such

The Artist

quantities of alcohol, but I felt exhausted. Drunkenly, I checked my wallet, dropping it in the process, but it contained no notes. I could feel a pile of loose coins in my right pocket, but upon inspection it did not appear to be enough to pay for a cab. I would have to walk again, and this time I didn't think I'd make it. The idea of sleeping out on the grass, a little way along from the pub, crossed my mind, but I was too terrified of rolling over the cliff edge in my sleep. So, I started walking.

Now, there are two fairly direct routes from the Traveller's to my home. The safest, and the one I always take, is to simply follow the main road for a couple of miles and take just one turning off of it. At a sober walking pace, it is around a thirty-minute walk, but in my usual evening condition, it can be anything from forty to fifty minutes. There is also a short cut, but as with any short cuts, it comes with a degree of risk. A pretty significant risk, actually, even if one were sober when attempting it.

The Artist

There is an area of coastline between The Traveller's and my home, which would be described as treacherous. It is essentially a quarter mile of rocks and boulders, interspersed with rock pools, rusty shopping trolleys, and even a very old car which came over the cliff in the 1950s. However, it isn't merely the terrain which makes for difficult travelling. This stretch of coastline is on a curve, meaning that you simply cannot see around to the safety of the next beach until you are almost upon it. In fact, it is more like two curves, a soft 'w' shape, if you like. I remember reading the coast guards warning before, which explained that, even if you time it right, you only have about thirty minutes to traverse the rocks before the tide cuts you off. Although there are a multitude of warning signs suggesting that it would be unwise to attempt it, thirty minutes is plenty of time to make it across. At least, it's plenty of time if the tide is fully out, and you are sober and agile. On this evening, I was none of those things, and the tide, despite appearing to be out, was actually returning, in what seemed to be a hurry.

Now of course, choosing to take this short cut was a stupid idea, but stupid ideas seem to come to me often when I'm drunk, and drunk is something that I usually am. Having convinced myself the tide was far enough out, that I wouldn't have any issues with climbing across boulders in my work shoes (when walking in a straight line was more than a little challenging), and that this was a much quicker route home, I began the descent on to the rocks. I just hope that I wouldn't have attempted it if the moon wasn't providing such superb luminescence, but with the help of my mobile phone's flashlight app, I could see well enough. I didn't get halfway.

The tide had made its way back in, splashing gently against the cliff face in the central part of the soft 'w'. I wasn't happy, and considered swimming, before my brain reminded me that I'd certainly drown. Annoyed at having wasted more time trying to get home, I turned back, hurrying myself over a particularly large boulder, and looked ahead for the entry point. I could see the metal bars which signified the end of the promenade, the moonlight glinting off of the metal. Then panic gripped me. Between the promenade, and my position on the rocks, was nothing but seawater. The warnings from all those signs that I had chosen to ignore came to mind, and I began to tremble. I climbed on to a higher rock, looking behind me to see that the tide had risen another metre or so in the last few minutes. I had two choices; try to swim for it or call the coastguard. Even in the state I was in, swimming felt like a stupid idea, beyond even my own levels of foolishness. There was no telling how deep the water was, how strong the current would be, and there were all manner of threatening rocks beneath the surface which could do me damage. It would have to be a call to the coast guard, and a prayer that they arrived quickly. I fumbled with my phone, the

The Artist

flashlight pointing at my now green and slimy shoes. I pressed the '9' button three times. The operative answered, and I turned. I have a habit of pacing when on the telephone, and my brain had not warned my feet that now was not the time. I took a step, and before I could explain my predicament, my foot slipped from the side of the rock, and everything went black.

My phone was long-gone when I came to, so I couldn't have told you how long I had been out, even if the thought had entered my head at the time. What I do remember was the music, soft and rhythmic, as though being played on a harp, or perhaps a lyre. The tune was unfamiliar, and I must have been listening to its soothing melody for a few minutes before I even tried to open my eyes. There was another sound in the background, water lapping against stone. That's when it all flooded back to me; the drinks, the rock climbing, the getting cut off by the tide. But where was I? I'd clearly been knocked out from the

The Artist

fall, so I should have drowned. Unless the coastguard found me in time? I had a vague recollection of calling them, but did I even tell them where I was? The memory was too hazy to be certain.

I opened my eyes, half-expecting to be in a hospital, and the sounds to be my imagination, but I was not. It was dark, but not the wild darkness of night-time. There was no mistaking that I was in a cave or tunnel, but the walls glowed with a turquoise hue, reminding me of an episode of Blue Planet which talks about the phosphorescent creatures in the deep ocean. I looked to my left and right, seeing nothing but natural illumination on the cave walls which appeared to stretch as far as I could see in both directions. I closed my eyes, trying to focus my hearing. The music, if that is what it was, came from my right. The sound of water was not coming from my left or right and was unmistakably coming from *above* me.

The music, eerie as it was, seemed to call to me. I tried to

The Artist

stand, fumbling in the darkness, my hands pressing against the slimy walls for support. It was damp, but not cold, and I ran my hands down my now crumpled shirt and across my rear to discover that I was completely dry. This struck me as odd, but I couldn't quite establish why. I had to choose a direction and had no clue which way to go; the only noticeable thing was the music. However, music meant people surely, so it made sense to follow the sound. In the poor lighting, I continued to trip over rocks, splash in shallow pools, and run my hands over unpleasant feeling surfaces as I made my way. There was no way of telling how far, or for how long, I had travelled, but it felt as though hours had passed.

The music remained as clear as it had been when I first came around, but no louder. I wondered if my mind was playing tricks on me, or whether I had simply not made it far enough. I looked back for the first time, considering whether I should have gone the other way, but it appeared different. Darker than I remembered. Shadows seemed to move against the walls of what now was unmistakably a lengthy network of tunnels. I shivered, not through cold, but a hint of fear gripped me. Of course, I was already afraid; being lost and potentially trapped, in the dark is rather terrifying, but this was something different, something sinister.

Heading back felt dangerous, so I kept going, speeding up as well as I could on such terrain. I refused to turn around, certain that I could detect shadows moving in the far-reaches of my eyesight. Just when I thought that the tunnel had no end, the distance between the walls began to widen, weakening the reach of the phosphorescent light, and forcing me to choose a side. The music appeared to come from both directions, so I kept to the right, without much thought, as my hand continued to slide across the surface. Following the wall as it sloped further away from its counterpart, the music finally grew louder. I paused, the beating of my heart audible above the stringed

The Artist

instrument, and chanced a look around. I could make out the light from the wall I had left behind, snaking its way in a circular formation, finishing at the point at which I stood. I may have awoken in a tunnel, but I was most certainly in a cave now. I could just about make out the entrance to the cave which I had passed through, and a different kind of light near to it. I stared, trying to focus my eyes, certain that I had not missed a red light on my way through.

It was small, and I wondered if it was the light from a phone, or other electronic device. I strained my eyes, debating whether or not to head towards it, when I realised there was more than one red light. Six, in fact. And moving in pairs. Not just moving, but moving in my direction, shrouded in jet black shadow. I had to run, my fight or flight reflex told me as much, but the practicality of gaining any speed in a dark and treacherous cave meant I was unsuccessful. I felt cold as they approached, my hairs standing on end, my pupils dilating as I saw my demise approach. And then nothing.

There did not appear to be any time between that encounter and me suddenly standing on a candle lit, circular stone floor. It was as if I had simply been transported from one location to another, but I suppose I had been heading in this direction anyway. I studied my surroundings, trying to understand my situation a little better, but to no avail. I was still in the cave, but the turquoise light I had followed so faithfully now appeared perhaps forty or fifty feet above me. I was stood on a circle of stone, some thirty feet in diameter, but it was not a natural feature of the location. The stone was carved with intricate designs, none of which were familiar to me, although something about them made me uneasy. I wouldn't have known with any certainty if they were occult symbols, but this was the first thought that came to mind. In the very centre of the stone circle stood a robed figure, playing on an ancient version of a harp. I could not make out their appearance as the robe ran from head to foot, the hood largely obscuring their face. Even so, it was evident from the hands alone that the musician was female, with young-looking skin.

I glanced around once more, nervous about the return of those shadows, but saw none. I continued to stand there, not wanting to interrupt the music; something about the situation made me certain that I should wait to be spoken to. When she showed no sign of stopping playing, I had no choice but to speak.

"Where am I?" I asked. The music stopped abruptly.

"You are here," came the soft voice.

"Where is here?" I replied, a little irritated by the stupid answer I had been given.

"Home," she said.

"Your home?" I wondered, doubtful that anyone could actually live in a cave, no matter how mad they were.

"Our home."

The Artist

"Enough of the cryptic bullshit," I told her, my angry words seeming much louder than I had intended as they echoed from the damp walls of the cave. I thought I detected a sigh leave her mouth. Slowly, she placed the instrument on the ground and lifted the hood from her head. I was taken aback by how beautiful she was. She then proceeded to remove the fastenings beneath her chin, slipping the robe from her shoulders and allowing it to drop to the floor. I struggled to keep my mouth closed as I took in her full nudity.

"Erm, what's going on?" I asked, a little bashfully. "Who are you?" She took a step towards me.

"I'm The Mother," she said, her green eyes twinkling with something mischievous. Her red lips parted a little as she cocked her head to the side, almost playfully.

"Whose mother?" I was unsure if I wanted to know the answer to this. She ignored the question.

"My children saved you." I tried to remember what had

The Artist

happened but could recall nothing after slipping from the boulder I had been standing on.

"And where are your children now?" I asked nervously, trying to politely look at her face when speaking to her.

"They are around, playing somewhere, no doubt."

"I need to get home," I told her. As nice as it was to speak to a beautiful, naked woman (something I had not had the pleasure of for some time), the situation was too bizarre and unless it was all a dream, I knew it couldn't end well.

"Up top?" she asked, a glint of anger flashing across her face. I didn't understand at first, but quickly realised that we had to be beneath ground level.

"Yes, how do I get back there? I don't remember how I came into this place." She appeared to be thinking about my question.

"My children can take you back, if that's what you really want?" I looked at her, unsure of how to word my next statement.

The Artist

"Well, I can't very well just disappear and live in this cave with you!" I stated, as if it were the most obvious thing in the world, which I suppose it was. She looked displeased with my words.

"Very well. Just know that they will only take you back to where they found you. The tide is high, and you will be returned to that very place. I just hope you are an exceptionally strong swimmer. Children!" The woman shouted for her children, smiling as three pairs of red eyes seemed to float towards me, impossibly black shadows surrounding them. I stepped back, afraid of what they would do. "If you change your mind," she said, her smile returning, "just call out for me. However, if you do come back, I would have to insist that you stay."

Before I could answer, I was gone from that room, suddenly ice-cold, and unable to breathe. As promised, I had been returned to the exact spot that I had landed from my fall, now a good four metres below sea level. The tide pulled me back and forth, far stronger than I could fight against. The saltwater burned my eyes, so I scrunched them shut and tried to swim in the direction I believed to be up. I did not have the strength, and pure terror overwhelmed me. My chest felt as if it would explode as I tried to hold my breath. Eventually, I could hold it no longer and took in a lungful of seawater.

It is a natural impulse to want to survive, and I wasn't in a position to weigh up my options. I knew I was close to death and, clinging to some illogical hope that it would work, I called out. She had only referred to herself as The Mother so that was the word I used. With a lungful of water, and on the verge of unconsciousness, I could make no sound, but my thought was heard somewhere in that underground room. A fraction of a second later I was spluttering up seawater across the stone circle that I found myself lying upon.

"I'm glad you returned," she said with a smile.

The Artist

"I didn't have a lot of choice," I retorted. "And I don't intend to stay."

"I made your options clear to you," she warned. "Now you are wet through. Put this on." She handed me a gown, identical to her own, which she must have fetched knowing that I would return in this state. Reluctantly, I removed my clothes and slipped it on. She looked at me approvingly. "Now you are ready." She turned on her heel, walking to the far side of the circle. Standing above a carving of what looked like a doorway, with horned creatures around it, she closed her eyes and mumbled something indiscernible. I watched in surprise as the ground opened to reveal crude steps descending further into the earth. I followed, certain I had no option, and knowing there was no way out from where I stood.

Flaming torches adorned the walls of a narrow tunnel, and I kept a few paces behind, still shivering from the cold water, trying to avert my gaze from her naked rear. The tunnel began to twist and turn,

The Artist

heading off in different directions, until I had no idea which way would lead back. And then we were at, what I assumed, was our destination. It took me a few moments to understand what was happening; the candles were no surprise, but there were at least twenty other people sitting in the room, all of whom looked too old to still be breathing. I noticed that they all wore the same black robes except one; a single, red-robed person was seated at the front. They sat in rows, with a walkway between them, facing the far end of the cavern. At the end of the walkway was an altar of some kind, an undoubtedly satanic image etched into the sandstone above.

My first thought was that I would become a sacrifice; that some devil worshipping cult would cut me to pieces and bathe in my blood. No one looked around as we entered, and she whispered to me to remove my robe. I didn't want to, but was significantly outnumbered if this went badly, whatever this was. She took my hand, and we walked

The Artist

towards the altar, naked as the day we were born. As we stood before it, the red robe approached us, a decorative cushion in her hands. The hands were old, wrinkled and twisted with arthritis. On the cushion sat two rings, and the gravity of the situation hit me just as hard as the icy water had done not long ago. I was about to be married. We stood, in traditional wedding fashion, facing one another. She leaned in and whispered in my ear.

"You have to go along with it, or they will kill you." I nodded, not doubting that she was telling the truth.

"But why me?" I asked, before the ceremony could begin.

"You were available. We saved you, and now you need to save us." I had no time to ask any more questions, as the red-robed official began mumbling in an unknown language. I looked around the crowd to see everyone staring at us in silence. But the thing that struck me was that all the spectators were female; not a man in sight. It all felt too solemn for me to interrupt, as crazy as that sounds. I couldn't take in what was happening, and stood in silence, as though I were numb. Before I knew it, rings were placed on our fingers, and we were ushered through a small doorway into a tiny room containing only a bed.

"I need to know what the hell is going on," I said, once we were alone. I tried to keep my tone forceful, but not angry. My words came out feeble and frightened.

"I am The Mother, the chosen one. Until my children grow, I am the youngest, and the only fertile member of our kind."

"Your kind?" I repeated. The suggestion that these were not human sounded ridiculous at first, but I had been transported from one location to another in the blink of an eye, and those shadow creatures were certainly not of this world.

"We have survived for centuries, finding mates as and when our numbers dwindled. We have gone by many names over the years before now. Sailors called us sirens, telling tales of how our

The Artist

singing would cause them to crash their ships. This was never the case; we helped people who were in danger. We just asked for something in return."

"A husband? That's insane." Again, her eyes registered something akin to anger.

"Usually just a mate, to continue our line. I wanted more."

"So, what? We are supposed to live happily ever after in a cave full of old women, and just make babies?" As soon as I'd said it, it didn't sound quite as bad as I'd thought. "And what were those shadow things? You called them your children, but they were something else."

"Just lie down." My brain told me that I didn't want to, but other parts of my body suggested otherwise. She touched me, gently guiding me onto the bed. I told myself to just go with it, and then work out how to escape after, still clinging to the hope that this was simply a dream. As she had her way with me, not entirely against my will, she began mumbling in the same old language I had heard before. Her breath quickened, her face became flushed with red. I could feel myself reaching the end and, with her weight on top of me, knew there was no way to stop this happening. As I climaxed inside of her, she smiled, rubbing her belly.

"Those 'things', as you called them, are my children. The Children of the Deep. They are simply in our true form." The words seemed to take an eternity to be deciphered by my brain, but when they were, I knew I was finished. I must have looked frightened, or confused, most likely both, and she seized the moment to demonstrate what she meant. With a rush of air, her eyes went from that crystal green to deep red, her flesh transformed from pale white to a jet-black shadow, and she hovered above me. No other facial features were distinguishable on her, but my expression must have shown it all. That, and the rapid release of my bladder.

I attempted to roll from the bed, hoping my legs would hold out long enough for me to get away from

The Artist

whatever demon this was. I got as far as opening the door, only to be greeted by the red-robed one. I tried to shove her out of my way, but my actions triggered a terrifying scream from all twenty or so creatures. I heard my new bride beg for them to not harm me, to no avail. The room was now filled with shadows of other-worldly darkness, red eyes all directed at me. They were upon me in seconds, the shadows pulling at my flesh until it tore away in strips. There were so many of them that I couldn't see what was happening, but every part of my body felt on fire, and I was beginning to lose consciousness. I heard a voice, her voice, and they backed away. I looked down at my torso, my insides now hanging out in a bloody heap. I could taste blood in my mouth and struggled to breathe.

She put on her previous appearance, possibly to comfort me, as she knelt by my head, stroking my hair. She looked sad, disappointed perhaps, and for a fleeting moment, I felt guilty, as if I

The Artist

had let her down. As if this was all my fault.

THE CONFESSIONAL

Hypocrites, every bastard one of them. That's the way I saw it anyway, and the way anyone with any sense should be able to see it. I used to think that religion had its place. I used to think that it provided a crutch for people when times became tough. That was my youthful naivety, before I really started to think about things deeply enough. The looks of condescension, from people who seemed to only live to put others down, would make my blood boil. Divorced? You're off to Hell. Had sex or, worse still, a baby out of wedlock? Off to Hell. Got a tattoo? Said a fucking swear word? Had a beer on a Saturday night? No help for you.

Perhaps it wouldn't have been so bad if the ones banging on about the rules actually obeyed them themselves. With the exception, perhaps, of monks, everyone else of a religious persuasion was more than happy to criticize others. All the while, using their religion as an

The Artist

excuse for their racism, homophobia, and seemingly endless wars. And that's without even starting on all the child molestation that the church so willingly covers up. Eventually, it all got too much for me to bear and I had an overwhelming desire to rid the world of the parasite that religion had become, or perhaps always had been.

This wasn't an act of rage; at least not an uncontrolled loss of temper. I was angry, yet realistic, and never believed that I could bring down religion completely. However, I could certainly do something to terrify those that treated non-believers as though they were second-class citizens. And I would make a spectacle of it, that was for sure. And now here I am, sat in this confessional booth talking to you, Father. Your precious rules prevent you from repeating my confession, don't they? And now you'll hear about everything I did in all its glory. That's okay, you stay quiet and just listen.

The Artist

Four months ago, I caught my first one; it appeared fate had brought us together. You may remember seeing my work on the news? He wasn't a priest, or anything along those lines, but he helped at the local church so at least pretended to have some religious beliefs. Gerald, his name was. It came to light that his computer was filled with images of little kids, and the police stuck him on a register. Apparently too old for prison, he continued his life, minus Internet access, keeping his routine at the church. I went there one Sunday, to the church, and he was arranging the flowers. I spoke to the vicar after the service, something I struggled to stay awake through I must add, and he told me that the guy had 'repented' so all was fine. I hid my disgust as well as I could, but it must have shown on my face. I stood outside the church, watching the dirty old fucker talking to some kids, my hands balled into fists. He was to be my first.

I followed him home that day, to a small cottage on a quiet street.

The Artist

The front garden was well-kept, but as soon as the door opened I could smell the stench of piss and pipe tobacco. He had answered on my second knock and didn't appear to recognise me. He certainly didn't expect me to shove him on his arse and waltz into his home. He went down with a thud and I heard someone call his name. Now, this was unexpected; I'd assumed he lived alone and made a mental note to research my targets more thoroughly next time. An elderly lady poked her head around the door to what I presumed was the kitchen, her eyes suddenly widening as she saw me, and I hit her full force in the face before she could scream. She fell back, crashing into the mirror on the wall behind her and smashing it.

Gerald began to crawl towards me, his arthritic hands attempting to claw at my ankles, so I kicked him in the face and destroyed his glasses. He let out a whimper but stayed still. His wife, I don't recall her name, was sobbing and pointing into the kitchen. I think they might

The Artist

have had a tin of cash in there or something, as if this was a burglary! Yanking her hair back, my face an inch or two from hers, I asked her if she knew. Did you know what he had on his computer? I asked her as calmly as I could. She shook her head fiercely. I wasn't sure whether to believe her. How long have you been married? I asked. Fifty-seven years, apparently. That's a long time, wouldn't you say, Father. I'll take that grunt as a 'yes' shall I? And that's what I told her; fifty-seven years is a long time to be married to someone and not realise they are a dirty nonce. My money is on the fact that she knew, or at least had a suspicion. Maybe she was just a fucking idiot. Maybe she was stuck with him as you lot think divorce is a bigger no-no than kiddie porn. For a moment, I thought about letting her go, you know. But regardless of their ages, and putting aside whatever happy memories they may have shared, when he got caught she should have bailed on him. And that was her mistake. I picked up a piece of the broken

The Artist

mirror and sliced open her throat while Gerald looked on. He knew what was coming, and he knew why.

The press claimed that I stabbed him thirty-eight times, but that's nonsense. It was probably only about ten. Made a hell of a mess though. Blood poured from him, soaking the filthy carpet that he lay upon, and I watched as his eyes glazed over, a red bubble appearing from his mouth. Once I was content he was gone, I opened my bag and pulled out a can of spray paint. I sprayed the word 'pervert' a few times on the walls, changed my now rather bloody shirt, and walked out the front door, leaving it open. The press had a field day, and the general opinion was that the murders were carried out by an angry parent, or a now adult victim of Gerald. I hadn't been all that careful not to leave evidence at the crime scene, but no one saw anything, and I have no police record for fingerprints or DNA to be stored on.

How are you enjoying my story so far, Father? Still with us?

The Artist

Fine, don't answer, but I can hear you still breathing.

   Taking another victim so near to home would have been risky. Not that I planned to get away with it in the long run, but there was still a lot of work to do. I spent the two months after Gerald scouring the Internet for another person of interest. Not wanting to limit myself to merely killing perverts, I had to expose other facets of religious oppression. Then I found the perfect opportunity; a gay rights march. Usually that kind of thing wouldn't have piqued my interest, as a straight male. Now, I'm not claiming to be some hero of gay rights; I just don't give a shit what people are into if they are honest about it, and not hurting anyone else. After all, it's your words and actions that show whether you're a decent person or not, and where you choose to consensually stick your dick has no bearing on that. Which is something the Parents Against Pride group didn't seem to understand. Perhaps they do now.

The Artist

After a quick look through their Facebook group, which should certainly have been removed for hate speech, it was clear that the chief witch was strongly involved with her local religious organisation. She was the one arranging the protest against the march and, even more disturbingly, the one running the children's group to make banners for the event. It was too much to resist.

After an hours' drive, I arrived in the city which was hosting the march an hour before it was due to start. I'd seen the protesters plans online, and I was rather thrilled to find a pub opposite where they had arranged to gather. Taking a seat by the window with my pint of bitter shandy (I still had to drive back), I watched the group of about fifteen people gather, catching glimpses of their homemade signs. They were adorned with the usual homophobic slurs, I won't repeat them here, as well as the rather unoriginal 'It's Adam and Eve, not Adam and Steve'. My god, those people are idiots!

The Artist

Anyway, I'll cut the story short as I doubt you have all that much time left, Father. The parade marched on, largely laughing at the bunch of protesters, who became more enraged still. Once they had had enough, they dispersed to a nearby car park and I trailed along behind them. I had no real plan, so my next move was rather bold, and I'm sure influenced by a movie. Maybe movies do promote violence, huh? Although I was already of a murderous mind so perhaps that just helped me with the ideas? Who knows? Now, the woman in question, Pamela, had come alone on that day. Presumably her husband wanted nothing to do with it, or he had the sense to at least keep their kids away. That could be giving him too much credit; he could have been balls deep in Pamela's sister for all I knew. Whatever he was up to, it worked out well for him, and he's still alive and breathing as far as I know.

Pamela drove a car that was way too large for her petite frame; some monstrous 4x4 that she could

The Artist

barely see over the steering wheel in. It also turns out that she wasn't all that observant towards the back seat either, as I managed to sneak across it as soon as she pressed the unlock button, whilst she was busy exchanging nasty observations with one of her fellow Parents Against Pride. If I'd known that Pamela was heading straight home, I would have put together a better plan, but I really was winging it to begin with.

I remember lying on that leather back seat, certain that at any moment she would hear my breathing and I'd have to react quickly, but she did not. Twenty minutes later she parked up, outside what I guessed was her house. As we pulled into a space on the street, I withdrew the cheese wire from my jacket pocket. She turned off the ignition and I struck, quickly lifting it over the headrest and pulling it tight against her throat. Her legs kicked, but the more she pulled against the wire, the deeper it cut. I pulled the handles in a sawing motion, feeling the movement become easier as the

The Artist

wire moved below, through the skin. Even after Pamela had gone limp, I kept at it, almost decapitating her. As quietly as I could, I retrieved the same can of spray paint I had used at Gerald's, wrote 'homophobe' on the side of her car, and disappeared down a side street.

Are you still conscious? I don't hear anything; hang on, I'll come around to your side. Jesus Christ! Look at the state of you! Hello? You still in there? Well, there's a pulse so I'll just assume you can hear me. Where was I? Oh yeah, Matthew and the sanctity of marriage. I guess it's true about those who doth protest too much. This guy was real bastard. Okay, picture this: Matthew was a speaker at an evangelical church, one of those super lively places that insist on the reality of miracles and seem more popular with the youngsters. His specialty subject, the one he banged on about at any given opportunity, was marriage. And, unsurprisingly, his view of marriage was based on religious teachings. Marry once, don't get divorced, the wife is to be

The Artist

obedient, and so on. Not very modern, but neither is the church. As I explained, (I hope you got that), my issue is with the hypocrisy more than some outdated belief system. So, imagine my surprise when I found out that Matthew was married, not to his second wife, but his third! I did a bit of digging, and marriages one and two ended following claims of domestic violence and sexual assaults. I guess the previous wives were not as obedient as Matthew had wanted! And the third, Penny, was going through the same ordeal, she just hadn't had the courage to leave yet. But it was okay, because I would be setting her free very soon.

    I paid her a visit when Matthew was at work, having knocked up a fake ID and claiming to be from the local authority. I told her we had received reports of suspected violence against her and wanted to check on her well-being. She accepted what I told her as truth, breaking down in tears almost immediately. We talked for some time that day, and I was

The Artist

overcome with a feeling of compassion as I listened to her problems, promising that nothing would be said until she was ready to do so. I told her about Matthew's previous wives, and she was shocked. She thought she was his first, both in marriage and in the bedroom. Penny admitted that, at times, he had been rough with her, but did not realise she had been sexually assaulted. Poor girl was so naive. She told me that sometimes she would say no, and he'd climb on anyway, but she thought that was how marriages worked; Matthew had said so. I was trying to control my anger, to appear to be the professional Penny thought I was. I gave her the phone number for the Domestic Violence Hotline and said my goodbyes. She made me promise not to tell anyone, and I agreed. Of course, I'd be telling Matthew, but he wouldn't be repeating anything.

By this time, I had developed quite a taste for the killing, and before you say anything, I know it's a bit wrong. But I never proclaimed it as a sin and then went about

The Artist

doing it; I'm not a hypocrite. The media had picked up on the connection between Gerald and Pamela, but my message didn't seem to be being understood. So, I ramped it up a notch with Matthew. He was a big fucker, and from what I'd discovered, he was likely to be quite handy with his fists. I can't pretend to dislike violence obviously, but I'm not all that good in a fight. This was going to be harder than bumping off a couple of pensioners and a woman. So, I drugged him. It wasn't anywhere near as difficult as you'd think. I waited by his car, which was in his workplace's car park, and when he came over, I jabbed a needle in his neck. It was only morphine, which I'd had lying around at home after some surgery a while ago, but it did the trick. I shoved him into his car, and drove away, finding a quiet spot in the countryside.

Before he came to, I bound his wrists with cable ties, kept the seatbelt on for a bit of extra protection, and pushed one of his socks into his mouth as a gag. There

The Artist

were no people around for miles, but I didn't want to risk him screaming. This time, I had the chance to tell him exactly why I was there. Are you wondering why *you're* in the state you are? I'm sure you know, Father. We'll get to that soon. Anyway, I had Matthew in the passenger seat of his car, hands tied, mouth gagged. He looked bloody terrified when he woke up, but I suppose that was to be expected. He lashed about as much as he could, but it wasn't any good, and once he had calmed himself a bit I started to explain.

I told him that I knew about his previous wives, that I knew how he had treated them, and was now treating Penny. You should have seen his face when I told him I'd been to see her; that was a look of real anger. He was trying to talk to me, but I didn't take the gag out. It would have been bullshit anyway and I'm sure it would have made things worse for him. You could say I did him a favour by not listening. Now, this bit is important, and something I failed to get across to Gerald and Pamela. I explained to

The Artist

Matthew that whilst hitting your wife, and sexually assaulting her, is a pretty fucked up thing to do, under normal circumstances I would have just reported it to the police. What brought us to this situation was his constant preaching about the sanctity of marriage. I asked if he understood and he nodded rather enthusiastically. I suppose he would have agreed with anything I'd said at that point. So, I told him that the punishment needed to fit the crime. I remember that puzzled look on his face, as I unzipped his trousers and pulled out his dick. It was only afterwards that I realised he thought I was going to sexually assault him as a form of revenge, and by the way his dick grew I don't think that would have bothered him too much.

    I was pretty glad it grew so quickly, as I wasn't planning to touch it for any longer than necessary. I looked into Matthew's eyes, his dick in my hand, and felt a little awkward. I'm not sure what the look on his face was, but it quickly changed. I swapped my

The Artist

hand, now holding his boner in my left, reaching for the switchblade with my right. He knew what was happening as soon as he caught sight of the metal. He let out a moan, his eyes widening as I held his bloody stump of a penis up in front of his face. Blood poured from the wound, soaking the foot well in front of him, and I sat in silence waiting for him to bleed out. It took seventeen minutes. I didn't have to hurry as we were so secluded, and I took my time redecorating his car. This time I had to switch to a black paint, as Matthew drove a bloody yellow car! I mean, that is almost a reason to kill him in itself, surely? As neatly as I could manage, I sprayed the word 'rapist' on the car roof, 'wife-beater' on one side, and 'hypocrite' on the other. Then I retrieved his cock from where I had left it on the dashboard, threw it into some bushes, grabbed my bag, and began the long walk back to supposed civilization.

I spent the next few days checking the papers for any news, and when the story finally broke,

The Artist

one smart policeman seemed to understand my motive. Here, I have the article with me and I'll read you a bit. *We believe, following the most recent crime scene, that the killer is targeting those he, or she, believes to be acting in a hypocritical way. All the victims have been linked to religious organizations, and all have been involved in dubious activities. Currently, it is unclear whether the perpetrator is also of a religious persuasion and trying to remove the 'bad apples' from the church, but that is a theory we are working with.*

Well, if they are looking in religious groups then they won't find me there! Ha, although I'm currently sitting in this church with you, so that's an interesting thought. However, I can't see the police raiding this place any time soon. You don't look like you've got long left, Father. And you're getting blood all over the nice wood. Did you know, I thought about crucifying you, but it seemed a bit over the top. I'm sure when they find you with your guts hanging out then that will be adequate. Right! One

The Artist

more confession, then I'll leave you to it. This one is yours, so you'll want to pay attention. Don't worry though, I don't expect you to say anything.

We've met before, but I doubt you remember. Well, we didn't talk to each other so it's fine, but I was at the shelter last week. The one where you were taking that donation and getting photographed by the press. It irritated me, that you could be after the praise for making a charitable donation. I'm pretty sure that's a sin, isn't it? But I haven't killed you for that. I did a bit of digging, wondering what skeletons would fall out, and you didn't disappoint. Well, you did in a way, but you didn't surprise me I should say. So far as I can tell, you aren't a nonce, so that is a big plus for you. But you are a greedy little fucker, aren't you?

You own three cars, right? That's a rhetorical question. And a pretty big house for a priest's salary. Convincing the poorest people to throw ten per cent of their money into your collection pot is one thing,

The Artist

if it actually goes to a good cause, but pocketing it yourself is pretty low, even for a man of the cloth. You still there? Let's see how the old pulse is going. Hmm, can't find it Father. Fuck! Guess it's bye-bye for you. You don't mind if I decorate the side of this lovely mahogany booth, do you? I was going to write 'embezzler' but we're short of space. I guess 'thief' will be fine.

Then I'll be on my way, I promise. I'm sure it won't be long before the police are knocking at my door and I have a few more people to visit. Maybe I'll start a journal, so that when I am caught I'll have the chance to get my side across. Perhaps even a bestselling novel? People love reading all that grisly stuff. I just need a title. Don't be a fucking hypocrite! sounds a bit shit. Practice what you preach is better. Ooh, Righting their wrongs. I like that one.

The Artist

MEREDITH

Meredith O'Brien's house was a small one; a red-brick construction built to last. Nearly ninety years on, and it was almost as solid as the day it had been built. The only structural change in all this time had been to move the toilet indoors, and this had been put-off until Meredith's husband, Bill, had become too ill to trudge to the outhouse each time he felt the urge. That had merely been a decade ago, and Bill had struggled on for another four years before the prostate cancer finally took him, leaving Meredith alone. Living independently after almost sixty years of marriage took some adjustment, but Meredith found it to not be anywhere near as unpleasant as she had expected.

Of course, there was sadness, she had lost her husband, but she was not one to mope, and certainly had no intention of joining him any sooner than necessary. They had been unable to have children, and

The Artist

most of their friends had either moved away or been cremated by this point, and so Meredith passed her time painting, and writing the novel she had always dreamed of completing. Life was peaceful, and this was how Meredith liked things. She still found herself talking aloud, on occasion, with comments that would have been aimed at Bill, if only he could hear her. Meredith took pleasure in reading each completed chapter from her armchair, as if reading to a keen listener rather than her empty house. Life would have stayed this way too, if it wasn't for those bastard developers.

Once a week, Meredith left the house to shop for groceries, carefully planning what she would eat so as not to have to go any other days. This was always on a Friday morning, after breakfast, and before she sat down to add to her piece of fiction. The small, red-brick house was one of only four properties which had remained homes on that street; the rest gradually being renovated and marketed as retail premises. Meredith was a frugal woman and had no interest in the shops that had sprung up along her little street over the past few years. Food was a necessity, a bottle of Mother's Ruin was a treat once a month, but she needed little else.

Her lack of interest in the opening of other businesses meant that she did not notice when they began to close, either. Until, one rainy Friday morning, she couldn't get her groceries. The shop's windows were whitewashed, with no sign of life. Of course, there had been a closing down sign in all the windows for weeks before it had actually happened, but Meredith never took the time to read the signs. All that remained was a small poster displaying the address of the nearest store. The rain was becoming heavier, and Meredith could not remember the last time she had ventured farther than where she currently stood. Bewildered, she ventured to the end of the street and glanced in all directions, hoping it would not be too far to go.

The Artist

An hour later, Meredith dragged her tartan shopping trolley through her front door, removed her soaking coat, and slumped into an armchair to think. She didn't like the shop she had found; it was expensive, farther away, and the people working there couldn't speak English. She scolded herself a little for her casual racism but could not deny that she found it irritating being unable to understand what the staff were saying to one another.

Unaware of any other options, Meredith resigned herself to the same journey on the following Friday. She was thankful that the weather was far more pleasant this time and made a conscious effort to take in her surroundings. She lived exactly half-way along the street. There were twelve properties for her to pass as she headed towards the junction at the end of the road. Nine businesses, including the grocery shop, all had either closed signs in the windows, whitewashed windows, or heaps of mail visible through the glass doors. There were three houses and, despite the lack of any

The Artist

sold signs on display, they looked long-since abandoned.

"This town is really going downhill," Meredith mumbled to herself, hoping the new shop would have some decent gin, and feeling desperate to get home.

Almost four weeks passed, the days filled with the usual routine, until there came a knock at the door. Three hard knocks, in fact, which caused Meredith to jump a little, and adding too much paint to the brush she was holding.

"Who on earth could that be?" she mumbled. No-one ever came to visit, there was no-one she knew well enough. Meredith's first thought was that it could be someone selling something, either tat she didn't need, or a religion that she had no interest in. In which case, it would be simpler to ignore the caller. *Surely there are too few homes along here now to justify sending out salespeople.* Meredith pondered. *Or someone needs help?* A little reluctantly, she made her way to the door and opened it, letting out an audible sigh. She was

The Artist

greeted by two overweight men in suits, both wearing lanyards, one holding a clipboard.

"Good afternoon Mrs. O'Brien. My name is Patrick Matthews, and this is my colleague, Daniel Smith."

"I'll stop you there," Meredith began. "I have everything I need, both physically, and spiritually."

"We're not here to sell you anything," Smith interjected. "We're following up on the letter that we sent you some months ago, regarding your house." Meredith's face was blank.

"Did you not receive our letter, Mrs. O'Brien?"

"I don't open my mail," she explained. "No-one writes to me, my bills are all paid, and everything else is junk."

"I see," Matthews said, looking a little nervous. The letter would have given some warning, but now he had to do it himself. "You have probably noticed that the other properties on this street have closed, the homes are empty?"

The Artist

"I'm aware of that. I have to walk farther to get my shopping now, and I'm not happy about it."

"Sorry to hear that. We represent the firm which has purchased the properties on this street, with a view to developing the land. Due to the generous offers made, we have had no difficulty in obtaining them all. Except yours, Mrs. O'Brien." Meredith stared at the men for a moment, processing what she had heard.

"My house is not for sale, if that's what you're getting at?"

"We are aware of the market value, Mrs. O'Brien, which has dropped since the closures of the businesses around you. We are willing to offer you fifty per cent over and above that value."

"I don't care if you are offering one hundred times the value; the house is not for sale. I'm too old to be moving house now, I have enough money for myself, with no-one to leave it to if I had more. I'll be in this house until they take me out in a box." With that, Meredith closed the front door, and headed to the kitchen to fix a large gin. Her hands shook as she poured a triple measure into the tumbler, hating confrontation but angry at the audacity of the developers, and upset by the thought of her home being demolished. Despite having stated her position clearly, Meredith had a niggling suspicion that they would not give up quite so easily.

Two days had passed before Matthews and Smith returned. Meredith tried ignoring the banging at the door, but they were persistent, and she had had enough.

"I've told you I'm not selling," she stated, before either man could speak.

"We understand that, Meredith. May I call you Meredith?" Smith began.

"No, you may not," Meredith snapped back.

"Apologies. We have discussed the conversation we had last time and feel able to make you a substantially higher offer. Now, I know..." was as far as the conversation went before Smith found the door closing in his face. Instinctively, he placed a foot against the door frame, preventing it shutting completely. Meredith tried to hide the fear from her face as she took a step back, focusing on the feeling of anger instead.

"If my husband was still alive, you wouldn't get away with this behaviour! Now move your foot before I call the police!"

Matthews nodded at Smith, who slowly retracted his foot. No sooner had he moved it than the door slammed shut, seemingly of its own accord. Meredith stared at the door, trying to convince herself that, despite the stillness in the air, it had blown shut.

"Stupid woman," she heard one of them say. "Looks like it's Plan B."

Plan B? Meredith wondered. *Offer more money? Send in the heavies? Do people really do that? Well, I won't be bullied out of my home.* The return of the two men had set Meredith on edge, and she double locked the front door as a precaution against their return.

The Artist

Jason sat in greasy cafe cradling his coffee as he awaited his employers. It was shady business, but he'd been doing their dirty work for years by this time, and never considered quitting. The money was good, as with most illegal employments, and he took a certain pleasure in completing each task. He glanced towards the door as the two suits walked in, taking the seats across the table from him.

"What you got for me?" Jason asked. Matthews slid a scrap of paper across the sticky table, an address written on it.

"The boss needs this place. But the owner won't sell."

"How many in the house?" Jason asked.

"Just her; Meredith O'Brien. She's old, got to be more than eighty. No interest in money, says she's too old to move. Stubborn woman."

"OK," Jason replied, downing the last mouthful of cold coffee and standing to leave.

The Artist

"Whatever it takes," Matthews told him, grabbing his arm. "We need her out within the week." Jason leaned towards Matthews' face and grinned.

"Take your fucking hand off me, unless you want to lose it." Matthews withdrew his hand, keeping eye contact with Jason.

"Just do what we pay you for." And Jason was gone.

Meredith rarely looked out on the street, preferring the view of her small back garden, which her painting room provided her with. This meant that for the rest of the day, Jason could observe the house from his car without being noticed. He clocked a few lights coming on and off inside, confirming that the owner was at home. He noted in his small notebook that she did not leave the house on that day. Once it was late enough to assume that Mrs. O'Brien would be sleeping, he approached the front door and gently tried the handle. There was no room for movement and hoping that the coast was clear, he shone a

The Artist

torch between the door and the frame. *Double-locked. Shit.* On the left-hand side of the house ran a narrow pathway, leading to the side entrance of the building next-door. A building that had once been a home, then a Polish food shop, and now sat empty. Carefully, Jason side-stepped past three plastic wheelie bins overflowing with rubbish. To his disappointment, there was no side door, or garden entrance, to Meredith's property. There was, however, also no lighting at the back of the property, and he was completely hidden from sight. The garden was bordered by a fence, approximately six feet in height, but certainly scalable.

Keeping his torch off, Jason pulled himself over the fence and slid quietly onto the flower bed that ran the length of the garden, destroying a couple of pansies on the way. The house sat in darkness, and he could just about make out the white uPVC frame of the back door, which led from the garden into the kitchen. He tried the door, on the off chance it had been left unlocked, but no such luck. He decided to call it a night once he had left his mark in the garden. After Jason had pulled up every flower that he could manage, kicking dirt across the lawn, he turned his attention to the ornaments, knocking them over, or simply flipping them upside-down. All the while, he could not shake the feeling that he was being watched. This kind of nocturnal, criminal activity was not something new to Jason, and there was always a little paranoia about being spotted. However, this felt different, like there were eyes on him. It was as he turned to destroy the bird bath that he was startled by something moving; a shadow in the periphery of his vision. He looked around but saw nothing. As his foot connected with the bird bath, the shadow seemed to swirl around him for a second before disappearing. *Bastard cat,* he thought, optimistically. Cat or no cat, Jason was sufficiently spooked to be on his way.

The Artist

Meredith almost dropped her teacup when she looked out of the kitchen door on the following morning. Despite the garden being small, she kept it presentable. The grass area was kept tidy, the beds were always filled with seasonal flowers, and the ornate wooden bird bath (which Bill had hand-carved himself) sat proudly in the centre. That is, until now. Huge chunks of grass and soil had been ripped from the lawn, every single flower had been yanked out by the roots and, most upsetting of all, the bird bath now lay scattered in pieces. She had never experienced anything like this before and had no doubts as to who was responsible. Without hesitation, Meredith called the police, foolishly thinking that they would be able to catch the perpetrator.

"We will have a chat with the men who came by," the officer told her, with a look that said, *'Don't get your hopes up.'* "But there is a good chance this was just kids. In the meantime, keep your house secure and get in touch if anything else happens." The police gave the garden another quick look-over before making their exit, all under the watch of Jason, who was parked a few buildings down from the house.

Deciding to deal with the mess outside a little later, Meredith grabbed her shopping trolley and made her way out the front door, double locking it and trying the handle to be certain. She was visibly shaken, glancing up and down the street before she began the journey. *It has to have been those bastards,* she told herself. *Surely when the police confront them, they will back off.* From the crossroads, it was another ten-minute walk to the convenience store. She dragged her cart around, unable to concentrate on what she was really doing, not noticing the man who watched her from the end of each aisle. Once she had paid, and made her way outside, she did not notice him approach her from behind until he was inches from her face.

"You really should think about moving," he said with a grin. "At your age, people tend to have a lot of

The Artist

falls." Before she could reply, Jason was running ahead of her, disappearing out of sight. Meredith froze, attempting to process the threat she had received, unsure of what to do. However, it wasn't fear that she felt, as much as anger. *The police will have to act now!*

Meredith's pace quickened, as she hurried home to call the police. The fear that this unpleasant man could be waiting for her loitered at the back of her mind, but the idea of heading straight to the police station didn't occur to her. Reaching the door to her home, Meredith fumbled inside her handbag trying to locate her keys.

"For goodness' sake!" she muttered, slowly removing each item in her search. As she took out the last objects, a look of horror spread across her face as she realised they were not there. She knew full well that she had needed to use them to lock her front door, and the chance of them simply falling from her bag was virtually zero. Cautiously, Meredith tried the door, half expecting it to be unlocked and her assailant waiting within. However, the door remained firmly closed, with no way for her to gain entry.

For ten minutes, Meredith stood outside of her own home, weighing up her options, trying to hold back the tears that were forming. Taking the walk to the police station was her only choice now, but before she had taken a step, a car pulled up beside her.

"Having some difficulties, Mrs. O'Brien?" Matthews shouted through the open car window, barely concealing the smug look on his face. Meredith reacted before thinking, anger taking hold, and she marched towards the car, swinging her now empty handbag at the man. Her attack was met with laughter. "Calm down, love. This is all going to be fine." Matthews reached into his jacket pocket and passed Meredith a folded piece of paper. She opened it, staring incredulously at the cheque. It was a large sum of money, but she had no intention of accepting it and tore it to pieces in front of him, scattering the pieces in the breeze.

The Artist

"I'm going to the police. You've effectively stolen my home."

Matthews feigned a worried look.

"Fine. You can have your keys back. We give up." He handed the bunch of keys over which Jason had passed to him at the far end of the road. Meredith snatched them away from him, scuttling inside without noticing that there was one missing.

Meredith tried to predict how the police would act. After all, she had her keys back, and these bastards had, albeit unconvincingly, said they were giving up on their attempts to buy her home. *I should report it anyway; at least get it on record somewhere in case they return.*

"We'll get an officer out to see you, Mrs. O'Brien, but it may not be until tomorrow, I'm afraid." This wasn't the news that Meredith wanted to hear, but she remained polite and thanked the switchboard operator. She had rolled her eyes when advised to keep the doors and windows locked, trying to resist

The Artist

making a sarcastic comment about how she had planned to leave everything open for anyone to wander in. With a hot cup of tea, Meredith sat herself in the armchair and thought over the events of the day.

"They wouldn't dare to do this if you were still here Bill," she said aloud, her eyes falling on their wedding photograph, which sat on the mantel piece. "You'd take care of everything." Meredith could feel her eyes moisten, as she fought back tears. "Why did you have to leave?" she said, a hint of anger evident. A gust of wind caused the curtains to flap, startling Meredith. Certain the windows had been closed, she stood up, to find that they still were. She looked around the room in confusion, teacup still in hand. Meredith let out a yelp as the small cupboard door in the corner of the living room swung open. Transfixed she stood, rooted to the spot, as two scenic jigsaw puzzles appeared to fall from the space, followed by a very old Scrabble set. Then nothing.

The Artist

After a good ten minutes of not knowing how to react, Meredith put the events down to something explainable, despite the fact she could not fathom what. Only as she went to place the items back in the cupboard did she feel it, feel him, gently touching her arm. She flinched at the cold touch, but the familiarity of it was undeniable.

"Bill?" she whispered, trembling, and feeling a little silly for even thinking he could still be around. The Scrabble set moved. Meredith cautiously bent down to pick it up, but an unseen force knocked it from her hands, scattering the lettered tiles across the carpet. Feeling faint, Meredith sat back in her chair, staring at the floor as the tiles began to move.

First an 'I' took its place in front of her, at her feet, before being joined by more letters. Meredith's eyes widened as the words formed; I didn't leave, Merry. No-one but Bill had called her Merry, not ever. She had no doubt that he was there, but the shock was enough for her pass out where she sat.

The Artist

By the time she regained consciousness, more letters had been added, telling Meredith that Bill loved her. She watched as they shifted back and forth, unseen hands spelling out the words that he would keep her safe when those men returned. However, Meredith didn't care anymore. Having never been particularly religious, she hadn't expected there to be anything beyond the earthly life. Now she had no doubts that they could reunite in death, and she wanted nothing more than to join her husband.

"I want to come with you," she told him. "They can have the damned house." The tiles moved, more slowly this time as if Bill was unsure how to respond. 'Not yet', Meredith read, followed by 'not because of them'. She began to sob. "I'm ready, Bill. You have no idea how lonely I've been! What do you want me to do? Keep living alone, our conversations reliant on bloody Scrabble tiles?!" There was a pause, much longer than Meredith expected, as Bill was clearly

The Artist

thinking through their options. The tiles shifted purposefully. 'Revenge first'.

Bill was angry, that much was clear to Meredith. The threat she was facing had, through an unexpected series of events, caused her to want to die. The developers had essentially killed Meredith, whether it had been their intention or not. The tiles jumped about on the rug. 'Call them'. Meredith pondered Bill's intentions, doubting that inviting those men to the house would end well for them. "I can't," Meredith began.

Before she could speak again, a clatter from the kitchen startled her. Curtains and papers rustled in the living room as Bill moved about. She could swear she saw a shadow leave the room and head towards the kitchen. Hands trembling, heart racing, Meredith followed and found Jason stood in her kitchen.

"What the hell are you doing in my house?" Meredith demanded, trying to hide her fear. "I'm calling the police!" Jason lunged towards the elderly woman, grabbing her by the forearm and turning her back to face him.

"I'm only doing my job, lady. You'd be much better off just selling the house." Jason couldn't read the expression on Meredith's face, a mixture of fear and surprise, followed by a smirk of satisfaction. If he had seen what came from behind him, Jason would have understood, but the first thing he noticed was the warm sensation in the side of his neck. Jason's grip on Meredith eased a little as he raised his free hand up to the now wet area. Dabbing his fingers in the moisture, he examined his hand to see the unmistakable crimson of his own blood. He placed a hand on the kitchen counter to steady himself, as dizziness took hold. Jason did his best to see who was behind him, but the knife struck again, plunging into his side repeatedly until he gurgled his final breath, drenched in red from head to toe.

Meredith stared as her kitchen knife etched words into the wooden countertop. 'Call them.' She was afraid, not only of the men who

The Artist

wanted her gone from her home, but now of Bill. Such a level of violence was out of character for him, certainly whilst he had been alive, but death brings a greater degree of freedom. Attempting to keep her voice level, Meredith retrieved the crumpled letter from her wastepaper bin, and dialled the number.

"Mr. Matthews?" she began. "Meredith O'Brien." There was a moment of hesitation. *Probably wondering if his thug has been here yet,* Meredith thought.

"Mrs. O'Brien, what a lovely surprise. What can I do for you?"

"I wish to sell the house. But it needs to be tonight."

"Well, I can't pretend to not be happy about that. What brought on the sudden change of heart?" Matthews asked, unsure if he really wanted to know.

"I'm sure you can guess, Mr. Matthews. I'm too old for all this nonsense, and as much as I think that you, and your firm, are the lowest of all God's creatures, I'm not going to stay here worrying about what you'll do next. Bring your

The Artist

cheque book and a contract round, and let's get this over with." With that, Meredith hung up the receiver and returned to the kitchen. Gingerly stepping over the body on her linoleum flooring, taking care not to slip on the ever-increasing blood puddle, Meredith poured a large gin into one of her crystal tumblers. "The ball's in your court now, Bill," she said aloud.

Barely fifteen minutes later came a knock at the door, and Meredith was greeted by Mr. Matthews.

"Come in," she said, trying to hide her disappointment that he had come alone. "Your partner couldn't make it?"

"I didn't think it was necessary to drag him out; I'll call him when we are done. Where would you like me?"

"Living room," Meredith replied, nodding her head towards the nearest door. She followed him in, taking her position in the armchair, whilst he sat across the room from her.

The Artist

"It's a pretty standard contract," he began. "It states that you are happy to transfer the deeds for the property over to the development firm, at the price stated within. The only parts which need completing are your signature, and the date at which the transfer would take place. How soon are you able to move?"

"Tomorrow," she told him. His eyes registered surprise, but he certainly looked pleased that it could be so soon. "And I would like the cheque made out to the local hospital. They took care of my husband before he passed, so it seems like the right thing to do."

"The whole amount?" the man asked, a little uncertain. "Do you not need some for the purchase of another property?"

"Do you want to buy the bloody house or not? What business is it of yours what I do with my money?" Meredith fixed him with a glare, and he said no more, reaching into his case for the cheque book and a pen. Meredith folded the payment in half, sliding it into her

The Artist

blouse pocket, before signing the contract.

"Well, that wasn't too painless, was it?" Matthews said, a little smugly.

"Not yet," Meredith mumbled. Matthews stood to leave, the contract still firmly in his hands. "Oh, one more thing. Have you met my husband, Bill?" A puzzled look spread over his face. *Old bat's gone a bit senile,* he thought.

"Er, I thought you said your husband had died, Mrs. O'Brien?"

"Yes, he is dead, that's correct. Nevertheless, he'd still like to meet you." Meredith grinned at the man, who looked a little flustered. Before he could take a step, the curtains flapped again. Matthews managed to get as far as the doorway of the living room before being launched backwards by an unseen force, hitting his head against the fireplace.

"What the fuck?" he mumbled, looking up at Meredith. Matthews felt a weight on his chest, keeping him to the ground. He screamed for

The Artist

help, unable to understand his predicament.

"Screaming won't help, I'm afraid. All the buildings around here are empty, remember?" Meredith looked content as she watched on from her armchair. The fireplace had not been used for decades, but it was ornamental, complete with an antique basket containing a brush, shovel, tongs, and poker. Meredith watched as the poker appeared to float in mid-air, before slamming down into the wooden floorboard, piercing Matthews' hand and securing him to the spot. He let out another scream, but it became muffled as the tongs entered his mouth, snapping at his tongue. They were blunt, but Bill's ghostly grip was tight, and the gurgling sound which accompanied the spurt of blood signified the loss of Mr. Matthews' tongue. There was only a soft moan, as the poker was ripped back through the man's hand and appeared to be aimed at his genitals.

"There's no need for that!" Meredith scalded her husband.

The Artist

"Just get it over with, please." The poker moved quickly, aligning itself with Matthews' face, specifically above his left eye. He tried to wriggle his head away from under the weapon but could not get it to move far enough. Meredith watched as the front of Mr. Matthews' navy-blue suit trousers darkened with urine, only seconds before Bill dealt his death-blow. As quick as an arrow, the poker forced its way through eye and brain with a squelch. His right leg twitched momentarily, then all was still.

"I need to find a stamp," Meredith explained, rising from her chair, cheque in hand. The rather large payment was quickly sealed into an envelope, addressed, and stamped. "I'm going to post this, then I'll be back," she told Bill. The street was silent, to her relief, and she made her way to the end of the road as quickly as possible, where the nearest post box stood. The redness of the box reminded her of the scene inside her home, and for a brief moment she felt something similar to regret. *Too late now,* she

The Artist

told herself, knowing there was only one way in which this could end. Letting herself back through the front door, and removing her coat, Meredith took to her armchair for what she knew would be the last time.

"So, Bill, how do we do this?" No answer. The tiles remained still on the floor. "Don't wimp out on me now Bill, I thought you were going to do this?" Meredith sat upright, eyes glistening with tears as she wondered if she could go through with suicide. "Bill!" she pleaded, letting tears fall. A cushion rose from the chair that had recently been Matthews' resting pace and moved towards Meredith. She smiled, whispering a 'thank-you'. As she closed her eyes, feeling the soft fabric press against her face, she did not try to fight it. Her chest began to sting as her lungs failed to fill, her head feeling lighter, until she was no more.

Moments passed before she could see again, but now everything had a vibrant tone to it. She gazed into Bill's eyes as he dropped the cushion and kissed her fully. "Merry, my darling. I've missed you more than words could ever convey."

"And I, you William. But you never have to miss me again."

UNEARTHED

It was dark when I opened my eyes. Darker than I expected. I waited for them to adjust a little, patiently allowing them to observe the familiar shadows within my bedroom, but they did not. I kept still, only my eyes darting around. For the briefest of moments, I thought I had lost my sight, until the light on my watch-face told me otherwise. 1.47am. It was too dark. I reached for the duvet but was unable to find it. I turned onto my side, sliding a hand across to feel for my lover; it did not find her, instead striking something hard and rough. Without taking a moment to think, I rolled onto my back, reaching out to the other side; to what should have been the edge of the bed. Again, a hard, rough surface met my fingertips. Now I was awake. I tried to sit up quickly, unable to see the same rough surface barely six inches above me and grazed my forehead in the process. Fear had dilated my pupils, but the darkness remained impenetrable. I pressed the light on my watch, its meagre glow providing little assistance. Tentatively, I reached behind me to find the same surface. I slid down to what should have been the foot of my bed, my heels striking the end of my coffin. For this was surely where I was, entombed in wood. Without any cover the chill was noticeable, even on this summer night. My hands found their way down my side, confirming that I remained as I had gone to bed - naked.

Considering my circumstances, I had remained calm thus far, assessing my situation with deliberate thought. Nevertheless, try as I might, I could not recall anything that had led me to this place. We had gone to bed at around the same time as always, made love in the way that we usually did, and had fallen asleep. That was barely two hours ago. *Nothing suspicious, or out of the ordinary, had happened that evening, had it?* I racked my brain, trying to recall something which could constitute a clue, but came up

The Artist

with nothing. *Idiot! Perhaps trying to get out of here should be a priority?* I could have been anywhere, and the late hour drastically reduced the chances of anybody passing by, no matter my location. Air was a commodity not to be wasted, and so, against my natural impulses, I resisted the urge to scream for help. I suppose I was still in a state of disbelief, hoping this would turn out to be a prank of some kind, even though I could think of no-one who would go to such extremes. Gently, I pressed my hands against the boards to my left and right, trying to detect a weakness, but found none. I had enough space to roll over, but not enough room to get my head to where my feet currently were. Knowing that my legs were far stronger than my arms, logic told me to kick at that end, and so I did.

It felt like my only option, and I went at it hard, certain that my life may well depend on it. I cursed myself for refusing to wear bed socks, as the soles of my feet took in splinters and turned slippery with blood. Again, and again, I kicked

The Artist

with as much force as I could. The wood cracked eventually, but it was of little consequence. I remained unable to push the boards outward against the weight of the soil. My hope that I was merely nailed into a box disappeared as soon as I felt the damp earth on my toes and I knew, without doubt, that I was buried. If I was to escape then I would need to turn around, to be able to at least try to shovel the dirt with my hands. Six feet of wet mud would weigh a lot, I assumed, and I saw a good chance that I would be crushed under this weight. *It's either that or just wait to die. I have to find a way to turn myself around.*

The width of the box was greater than the height, so it made sense to try to turn that way, in a kind of forward roll manoeuvre. Tucking my knees up to my stomach as tightly as I could, I began to swivel my body around. My nakedness offered me no protection from the rough wood which tore against my right side. As soon as my head hit one wall, I doubted it would be possible to get all the way

The Artist

around; certainly not without causing some serious damage to myself. Regret came flooding in as I thought about how I had neglected my body, cursing this ring of fat around my waist. Pulling my knees in with all the strength I could muster, I let out a yelp as the soles of my feet made contact with the left side of the box, forcing my scalp to push against the right. I was wedged there, rough surfaces at both extremities, tears welling in my eyes.

I breathed deeply, preparing for what I knew was going to be almost unbearable, and dragged my feet behind me. I could feel them slicing open, but the lubrication of the blood made movement easier. As my feet moved, so did my head, sending a searing pain shooting across my scalp as I broke forth, now face-down, my head at the opening that my feet had made. Gently, I touched two fingers on to the top of my head; it felt wet and I was sure that I had left hair behind, matted into the wood. My head hurt more than my feet, but my hands were still intact, and they were what

The Artist

I needed now. *Dig!* I told myself. *It's the only choice.* I fumbled in the dark with my hands, beginning to pull the dirt into the box. It moved easily but was wet and heavy. I felt things crawling between my fingers; the creatures that dwell in the darkness.

The earth did not fall in on me and, one handful at a time, I managed to move it. Trying as hard as I could to ignore the pain, I shovelled lumps one by one into the box, filling the space I left behind me. Only once did I stop, tempted to give in to the exhaustion, beginning to doubt which way was up and which was down. I checked my watch; it had been almost an hour since I had awoken. I had no idea how long I would have sufficient oxygen for, but I guessed it wouldn't be much longer. My breaths were coming harder and faster. I pulled at the dirt above me once more, one scoop, two scoops, then I hit something. It felt hard, yet movable; a root perhaps. The hope that I was nearing the surface propelled me on, until my eyes detected a glimmer of

The Artist

light peering through the split soil. It was the top, and I was going to make it.

I pushed a hand through, feeling the cold air hit it. My other hand quickly followed, both of them frantically pulling open a large enough space for my head to fit through. Fresh air rushed into my oxygen-starved lungs, my eyes adjusted to the moonlight, and I laughed. I was in agony, not just in my scalp and my feet, but my entire, naked, body had been scraped and scratched during my ascent. *It will heal, I just need to get home.* Using the last of my strength, I pushed against my mangled feet to climb out of what was almost my tomb, and lay face-down, unclothed in the wet grass.

"Holy shit!" I heard, barely able to move my head. *Help is here. I'm going to be OK.*

"He's fucking climbed out!" came a second voice. My brain took a split-second to process what I had heard. *He's climbed out. They knew I was down there. That voice is familiar.* I began to roll over, trying to see who was there. A man whom I did not recognize stood over me, looking me up and down.

"All that for nothing," he said, almost admiringly. He turned to face someone else. "I'll take care of it."

The pain that the rest of my body felt made the attack feel almost numb; I saw a glint of steel in the moonlight, and then I couldn't catch my breath. My chest began to feel warm and sticky, as my opened throat gushed red across it. I couldn't process what was happening, or why, I just knew it was over. I looked away from my killer, turning my gaze in the direction of the familiar voice and saw her. I'd hoped she was safely still in our bed, but that was not the case. She watched the life drain out of me, no sign of remorse on her pretty face, and I was gone before I could even guess at her motivation.

WASH AWAY YOUR SINS

"What the holy fuck has happened here?" P.C. Smith asked, yanking up the garage door. The stench of blood and piss was overwhelming. His colleague, P.C. Hawkins, gave the scene a quick look around, before vomiting on the floor. They had been responding to a call about what was only described as strange noises coming from the garage. Smith had assumed some kids had broken in and were drinking, or getting high, and hadn't hurried along to the scene.

"Guess we should have got here a bit quicker," Hawkins said.

"Keep that thought to yourself," Smith responded, giving his partner a stern look. He pulled the radio from his belt and called for backup.

Shortly, the garage was swarming with police.

"Boss," one of the P.C.s called out, directed at the lead detective. "You should take a look at this." He handed her a couple of sheets of

The Artist

paper. "Seems to be a confession, or something." The D.C.I. snatched the papers and headed outside to smoke whilst she read them.

If you are reading this, then I finally put my plan into action. There will, no doubt, be a lot of speculation as to what took place, and why I have done the things I have done, so here is my attempt to explain. I knew this day was coming; it had been on the cards for some time. For years, I had wondered what event would cause me to finally snap, pondering who would push me over the edge. My anxiety had worsened over the last few years, to the point that I dreaded each new day, fearful of phone calls, emails, even what came through the post. I became a recluse, only leaving the house when absolutely necessary, terrified of human interaction.

For months, I tried to convince myself that things weren't as bad as they seemed, that I simply felt this way due to a fear of abandonment, and what the doctors had called high-functioning anxiety.

The Artist

Nevertheless, just because you're paranoid, doesn't mean they aren't after you. It's very hard to say if the way I have been treated by people has made me feel this way, or the way I feel has made them treat me badly. Either way, the day has finally arrived.

Since my teenage years, I had no doubt that when I did leave this world, it would be at my own hands. I have always been OK with this fact. The overbearing sense of loss as I watched my family disown me, and partners leave me, brought me close to the end on numerous occasions. However, something else is there now, something more than sadness and feelings of inadequacy. Anger has found a place, and if I'm going to make the great escape, I'm not going to go alone.

For the last three weeks, I have been plotting and scheming something elaborate, a revenge that would shock all who read about it. The idea came about after I had received a string of abusive text messages; I have left my phone unlocked at what is now certainly a

The Artist

crime scene, so that this can be verified. I came close to ending my life that day, slicing at my arms and legs with a scalpel after finishing almost a litre of whiskey. I broke down, seeing my own weakness for what it was, and felt overcome with a basic human need for revenge. We may now live in a supposedly civilised society, but in older times it was reasonable to strike down one's enemies. In this, I had a certain advantage; I had no intention of getting away with murder.

These past weeks have felt as though I were on autopilot, putting together the events which, if all went to plan, culminated in the bloodbath that you have discovered. I wondered several times if I was a psychopath, thoughts of torture filling my mind, but realised that I am not. I knew I would find the actions difficult, but saw them as necessary, and a punishment fitting the crime.

I began by writing down the names of those who had wronged me, even in the slightest of ways. It wasn't as long a list as I had expected, and I thought very

The Artist

carefully about the actions of each person when I had reduced the list to the final three. As you will see from my phone, I contacted each person with a detailed explanation as to how I felt, giving them the opportunity for reconciliation. One chose not to reply, two only made things worse for themselves.

Two of my targets, for I refuse to call them victims, lived alone so were easier to secure than the third. Toxicology reports may still show signs of Rohypnol in their systems, but I doubt that the puncture wound from the hypodermic needle will still be evident. It is easy enough to obtain drugs and the necessary paraphernalia on the streets of this dirty town, and I simply knocked on each person's door, struck out with the needle, and loaded them into my car. They weren't small men, but I was strong, physically, at least. I was fast, and under the cover of darkness, no-one suspected a thing.

The third was harder, but not by much. I suppose it was fortunate that they all knew each other, so a simple text message requesting some company was enough to draw her out after dark and into my waiting arms. She should have stayed with her family, she should have put them first instead of running to, what she thought, was a more exciting choice. But some people are just shit.

The Internet provided conflicting information as to how much Rohypnol to use, so I went higher than the maximum suggested dose. If they were to wake up early, the consequences could have been far worse than if I had accidentally killed them prematurely. As a result, it took several hours for the men to regain consciousness, and another two for her to awaken.

If this was a movie, then I'm sure I would have built an elaborate kill room in some disused warehouse, but these places simply do not exist around here. The only places available to me were my own home, and the garage that I rent several streets away. As you will know by now, I opted for the garage as it is a little more secluded. Further from other people, but hardly soundproof.

The Artist

As soon as the first started to stir, I was on him, scalpel in hand, and took his tongue. I gagged a little at the feel of the wetness, frightened it may slip into his throat and cause him to choke. The benefit of rendering him silent was two-fold, not only was he unable to scream for help, he also had no way to try to talk me out of what I was going to do. I had my doubts as to whether or not I could go through with it if someone began pleading for their life.

For two hours I sat in that garage in silence, the two men bound with rope, wide-eyed and tongueless, staring back at me with a look of terror, and something else. Regret perhaps? As if they knew why they were there. One tried to move about, a strange grunting sound all he could manage, but I struck his hand with a hammer, and he became still. When she *started to murmur, I repeated the procedure, slinging her tongue rather unceremoniously on the garage floor with the others.*

Once she calmed down a little, which I'm sure was difficult under the circumstances, I began to

The Artist

explain. This is the part I had been looking forward to; a chance to say how I felt, how I had been wronged, without them being able to argue back or walk away. And so, I did. I reminded each of them how they had lied about me, how they had tried in every way imaginable to destroy my life, how they had made me feel. Their fate was apparent to them now, and their expressions appeared to alternate between defiant, remorseful, and confused. But I had said my piece, and it felt as though a weight had been lifted. In fact, I almost considered releasing them at this point. Almost.

On the drunken nights leading up to this moment, I had watched the most extreme horror films that I could find, wondering at the possibilities of using such extravagant torture methods. As I had felt queasy about the tongue removal procedure, I was now glad to have not gone for anything so gory when the time came. I needed something symbolic about the way their lives would end, and as most of their criticism of me had been based on their bizarrely

The Artist

interpreted religious beliefs, it seemed that my own version of holy water would be appropriate. If there really was such a thing as holy water, I have no doubt it would have scorched their flesh when exposed to it, due to the hypocritical ways they had lived their lives. However, in the real world, I would have to settle for acid. Hydrofluoric acid works well in TV shows at dissolving organic matter, but sodium hydroxide is the most practical. It is easily made at home with household equipment and can be stored in plastic bottles. I have some chemistry knowledge but was thankful to find instructional videos online.

I created enough sodium hydroxide to fill a plastic container, keeping it as concentrated as I could, and found myself holding the bottle as I looked down on my enemies. All I had really wanted was for them to love me, but they had pushed me to this. And now it was time for their god to save them, if he could. I explained my intentions, as clearly as I could, all the while watching the fear spread across their faces as the

The Artist

tears streamed down. I told them I held a bottle of sodium hydroxide, that if they were decent people, their god would protect them from its ferocity. I reminded them how they had brought me down in the name of religion, and that if they had been in the right, they would be perfectly safe and free to go. I suppose it was me looking for evidence as well, some proof of a higher power. Of course, I was more than aware that if their god chose to save them at that point, it would also validate the way they had treated me, proving I was nothing but a worthless creature undeserving of love.

I approached the first and, with rubber glove encased hands, I opened the bottle. He scrunched his face up in anticipation of the impending attack, perhaps hoping that the pain would be survivable. It would have been a mistake to think that. I poured around a third of the bottle onto his short, greying hair, and my holy water hissed on contact. He made strange noises from his throat as the acid dissolved a way through his hair, through his

The Artist

scalp, and bubbled away on his now-exposed skull. It must have been excruciating, but the acid was not strong enough to find a way through the bone and end his suffering. The others had turned away, unable to watch the suffering of one they actually cared about. I was sure they would have enjoyed watching if I had been the one in pain, even before my actions today. I peered down to inspect the top of the skull, hoping the reaction had merely been slowed, but there was no sign of my 'blessing' progressing on. Deciding that he had suffered enough, I picked up my hammer and landed three hard blows to the exposed bone, forcing shattered pieces to puncture the grey softness beneath, and ending his life.

Breathing heavily, the two captives stared at me, pleadingly, yet seeming to know their fates were sealed. They were to go the same way, almost. I wondered if the acid had lost some of its strength dissolving the hair and decided to take a slightly different approach. Unzipping the back hold-all that I

The Artist

had brought along, aware that it looked exactly like a serial killer's tool kit, I pulled out the large kitchen knife. Originally, I hadn't intended to use it, but I felt safer having it available. I took hold of her ponytail, pulling her hair back as firmly as I could, before slicing the skin from the top of her head and throwing the bloody lump of skin and hair to the floor. She passed out from the pain. I poured a generous amount of the acid onto the skull to weaken it, and dispensed of her with my hammer, just as before.

Two down, one to go, and I had no issue with prolonging the final kill. I had no attachment to my last target; he was a bully, and an all-round unpleasant person. The fact that the others seemed to adore him so much, rather than me, only made me hate him more. I thought carefully about his actions, which largely involved spreading horrific lies about me, both verbally and in writing. I already had his tongue, so his hands were next. With the hammer, I broke each finger until it was a bloody pulp, and he just watched. Whatever

The Artist

I did, he made no sound, didn't try to move, and seemed to be accepting his fate. I remember smiling sadly at him, as I decided to get this over with.

I took his eyes next, prising them out with the blade of the kitchen knife, and adding them to the pile of gore I was building. I slumped to the floor beside him, stroking his hair as I poured the remaining acid into the holes where his eyes had recently been. He twitched a few times, and then was still; I suppose that was a relatively quick way to go.

Now you know everything, in all its brutality, so the police investigating this scene will have an easier job to do. I can only apologise to whoever has to clear up the mess, but that is something I can no longer do anything about. As you may have guessed by now, the fourth body you will have discovered is mine. I opted for the gentler approach and have taken an overdose. However, this story is spun, if it makes it into the media, is of no consequence to me, but I do hope people will think about

The Artist

my actions, and maybe even treat each other a little more humanely.

Jesus Christ! She thought, extinguishing her cigarette. *At least it's an open-and-shut case.*

"Boss!" she heard someone shout, from inside the garage.

"What is it?"

"This guy, with the empty pill bottle. He's not dead."

Also available from the author

The Broken Doll

In a small town in southern England, a chance encounter triggers a catastrophic series of events from which no one will emerge unchanged. When Sebastian Briggs meets Ella, she needs his help. The type of help required, however, is far from what he had expected; dragging him down a path of lust and violence. As a married father of three, Sebastian must fight between his loyalty to his family and the desire he feels for another woman, a woman full of secrets and with sinister intentions. What begins as a simple conversation between two strangers soon escalates beyond any expectations, tearing apart Sebastian's home life and leaving death in its wake. The debut novel from Peter Blakey-Novis is a fast-paced tale, full of twists, crimes and steamy passion.

The Broken Doll: Shattered Pieces
After trying to outrun his problems, Sebastian Briggs is pulled back to his hometown to confront his past, with devastating consequences. Having to deal with his estranged wife, and the unstable woman who tore his life apart, Seb discovers that he is now a wanted man; the net quickly closing in with the threat of violence around every corner. Shattered Pieces is the nail-biting follow-up to The Broken Doll, bringing the twisting tale to a shocking climax.

Embrace the Darkness and other short stories
Step into the mind of the unstable, where nightmares become reality and reality is not always what it seems. Embrace the Darkness is a collection of six terrifying tales, exploring the darker side of human nature and the blurred line between dreams and actuality.

Tunnels and other short stories

From the author of Embrace the Darkness, Tunnels takes you on six terrifying journeys full of terror and suspense. Join a group of ghost-hunters, dare to visit the Monroe house on Halloween, peek inside the marble box, and feel the fear as you meet the creatures of the night.

The Artist and other short stories

The nightmares continue in this third instalment of short horrors from P.J. Blakey-Novis. The Artist and Other Stories includes a terrifying mix of serial killers, sirens, claustrophobia, supernatural powers, and revenge, guaranteed to get your heart racing and set your nerves on edge.

Grace & Bobo: The Trip to the Future

When Grace's teacher asks her to write about the future, it's the perfect opportunity to build her own time machine! Join Grace and her

The Artist

pet monkey Bobo as they set off on a thrilling adventure to a strange land and learn a valuable lesson from the creatures they meet.